This Walker book belongs to:

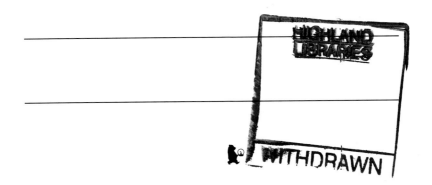

First published 2013 by Walker Books Ltd
87 Vauxhall Walk, London SE11 5HJ

This edition published 2014

10 9 8 7 6 5 4 3 2 1

This book has been typeset in Cochin

Printed in China

British Library Cataloguing in Publication Data: a catalogue record for this book is available from the British Library

ISBN 978-1-4063-5536-9

www.walker.co.uk

the mumsnet book of Bedtime Stories

TEN PRIZE-WINNING STORIES FROM MUMSNET & GRANSNET

HIGH LIFE HIGHLAND	
3800 14 0046908 0	
Askews & Holts	Oct-2014
JF	£9.99

WALKER BOOKS

AND SUBSIDIARIES

LONDON · BOSTON · SYDNEY · AUCKLAND

ABOUT THIS BOOK

The collaboration between Walker Books, Mumsnet and Gransnet to find ten bedtime stories by undiscovered writers was a new and engaging experience. Hundreds of would-be authors entered the competition, full of hope, and submissions ranged from the gently familiar to the quirky and original. The variety of talented new voices was impressive and choosing the shortlist of twenty stories was a challenging task. Once Michael Rosen had selected the winning ten from our shortlist, we commissioned ten new, young artists and asked each to illustrate a story. In this way we transformed each writer's vision. The collaborative experience has been profoundly rewarding for all involved and has resulted in a treasury of stories with something for every child. *The Mumsnet Book of Bedtime Stories* is a book for you and your family to share and enjoy for many years to come.

FOREWORD

Selecting the final ten stories in *The Mumsnet Book of Bedtime Stories* was a difficult task. The variety and talent demonstrated in the twenty shortlisted stories was impressive. How could I not include this charming fable or that rumbustious rhyme? In the end I settled on a range of different types of story in the hope that each one will not only give hours of shared reading pleasure but also inspire families to search out other stories and get into the habit of bedtime reading. A story shared at bedtime prepares a child for life. So, cuddle up with this book and get reading.

MICHAEL ROSEN

CONTENTS

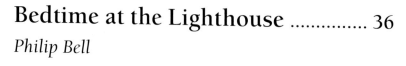

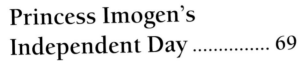

Time for Bed

Angela Eden

Illustrated by
Holly Sterling

"Time for bed," said Mama.

But that was NOT what Noah wanted to hear. He was busy playing behind the sofa. The yellow ball was so good at rolling, and the digger truck had such big wheels, and the bricks made a crashing noise as they fell down, and the drum made a loud bang-bang.

So he kept on playing. It was NOT time for bed.

"Time for bed," said Dada.

But that was NOT what Noah wanted to hear.
There was a mountain to climb up the stairs. He
held Dada's hand tight and tried the new walking
game. It was difficult to balance, stay upright, AND
hold hands AND get up each step. But he did it,
and there he was at the top of the stairs.

Now was NOT time for bed.

"Time for bed," said Mama.

But that was NOT what Noah wanted to hear.
He wanted to swim and slide and splash in the bath.
The green turtle was flapping its fins and gurgling under
the water. The water made a SPLASH as he poured it
from one cup into another. He wanted to sing the rowing
song, and then be wrapped up in a big towel.

He knew it was NOT time for bed.

"Time for bed," said Dada.

But that was NOT what Noah wanted to hear.
He wanted to play wriggle-giggle-catch-me on the big
bed. He wanted to roll about in his sleep suit. He wanted
to climb on the squidgy pillows, slide to the floor, and
play at being a tiger.

It was certainly NOT time for bed.

"Time for bed," said Dada.

But that was NOT what Noah wanted to hear.
He hadn't had his bedtime story yet. He wanted to
hear the noises the animals made, and count the fish,
and look at the trains going up the hill.

It was NOT time for bed.

"Time for bed," said Mama.

And maybe that
WAS what Noah wanted to hear.
This was the time for snuggling and
cuddling and one last drink of milk. It was time to
lie down and look at the stars on the ceiling and
listen to a bedtime song. He rubbed his soft blanket
against his nose and hugged his floppy monkey.
He felt warm and safe and SO sleepy.

It WAS time for bed after all.

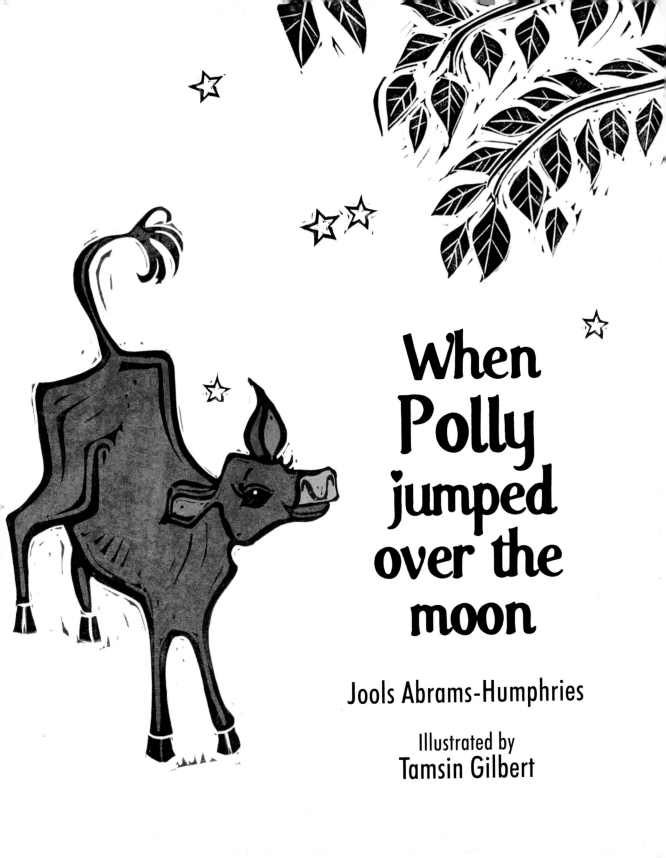

When Polly jumped over the moon

Jools Abrams-Humphries

Illustrated by
Tamsin Gilbert

POLLY WAS BORN one starry night under the old Hornbeam tree. Her mother was a Red Poll, her father was a Red Poll, and Polly was a Red Poll too. She wobbled around the forest on her unsteady legs, following the herd to the best grazing spots: over the plains and under the trees, by the lake and the coppice.

One day, as her head was bent low in the sweet grass, she heard some children playing. They danced under the old oak, skipping around the trunk with a small dog yapping at their heels, singing:

> *"The little dog laughed to see such fun, and*
> *the cow jumped over the moon."*

That night, as Polly snuggled up to her mother and looked up at the stars and the summer moon hanging in the sky, she began to wonder. She whispered, "Mum, can cows jump over the moon?"

Mum shook her head and laughed. "No, cows can't jump over the moon, Polly."

"I'm going to try," said Polly, and drifted off to sleep.

The next day, Polly practised jumping. She jumped over a little muddy puddle, and shouted, "I jumped over a puddle, Mum!"

Mum looked up from chewing the grass. "But cows can't jump over the moon, Polly."

Polly tiptoed over the cattle grid and ran back, leaping into the air. "I jumped over the grid, Mum!" she said.

Mum looked around from chewing the tree. "But cows can't jump over the moon, Polly."

Polly ran around the wood and jumped over a bramble ditch. "I jumped over the ditch, Mum," she said. Mum looked up from chewing the fence. "But cows can't jump over the moon, Polly."

Polly wandered to the edge of the forest, took a long run up and jumped over the stile. She shouted from the other side, "Mum, I've jumped over the stile!"

Mum looked over from licking the clover. "Well done, Polly – but cows can't jump over the moon."

Polly ran down the footpath.
She trotted past a hedge. Children
were flying up in the air, jumping
up and down.

"I can do that," thought Polly.
She waited until the children had
run back into the house, then she
pushed through the hedge and
climbed onto the trampoline.
Her little legs wobbled, but she
jumped, flying into the air, fields
and trees spread out before her.
"Mum, look at me, I'm jumping!"
she shouted.

Mum and the
rest of the herd looked up
in amazement. "Wow, Polly,
how wonderful!" said Mum.
"But cows can't jump over
the moon."

That night, back in the forest, the moon shone round and bright in the dark sky. Polly watched its reflection float across a clear puddle on the ground. She chewed on Mum's tail, and Mum turned around.

Polly took a long run along the muddy path, her hooves sliding in the soft ground, and leaped.

She jumped high in the air, gliding across the stars twinkling in the dark, right over the puddle, right over the moon.
"Polly!" Mum said,
"YOU DID IT!
You are the cow that jumped over the moon!"

THE **SHERIFF** OF **RUSTY NAIL**

Sophie Wills

Illustrated by **Alice Lickens**

MANY YEARS AGO, when railways had only just begun snaking their way across the vast land of America, there was a small town in the wildest part of the Wild West, and it was called Rusty Nail. There was no way to get to Rusty Nail except by riding for a very long time on a horse, and once you got there it was dusty and rickety and there wasn't a whole lot to do, so most people didn't bother. That meant the townsfolk of Rusty Nail were never visited by outlaws or other proper baddies, which they didn't mind one bit.

Now, there were a lot of cowboys living in and around Rusty Nail, with names like "Big Hank", "Sly Wade" and "Wiley Ranger", and they rode handsome, athletic and trusty horses in all shades of brown, white and black. And there was a sheriff, and his name was Brian.

Brian was very unusual in Rusty Nail, because he didn't own a horse. He was a quietly spoken man, and he didn't want to impose himself on any animal by sitting on its back. This was all very well until Big Hank and his friends began to mightily annoy the good people of Rusty Nail. They galloped their horses through the town at night, whooping loudly just for fun, and played naughty tricks like swapping over the sign for the barber's shop with the butcher's sign. This caused all kinds of trouble, though the town's chickens ended up with some very fashionable hairstyles.

Big, Sly and Wiley were so fast on their horses that even if Brian waited up all night to catch them red-handed, he could never hope to stop them. When he told them off the next day, they always said it hadn't been them.

So Brian decided he would have to get a horse. He went to see Belle Trotter, who sold horses, but she didn't have any left.

"There's a delay of six to eight months," said Belle.

"I can't wait that long! I've got to have something," said Brian.

But all Belle had was a very large pink pig. She had been going to sell her for bacon, but she said that Brian could take her for the same price as a horse.

Brian looked at the pig, who was a very different shape from a horse, being mostly round with four stout legs. He couldn't explain it, but he felt that she knew everything he was thinking.

"I can't let you be turned into bacon," he thought, and he bought the pig from Belle. "I shall name you Sarah."

When the townsfolk saw Sarah, they laughed and laughed until their Stetson hats fell off and the spurs on their boots jingled.

"That's the funniest thing I've ever seen," gasped Big, wiping tears from his eyes. "A sheriff on an enormous pig? Who ever heard of such a thing? And she's PINK! That's a girls' colour!"

Brian looked at Sarah. "If I put a saddle on you, I could ride you pretty well," he said.

"Just because nobody's done it before, doesn't mean I can't. And pink is not just for girls."

So Brian taught Sarah how to wear a saddle. She happily trotted along with him on her back, but it has to be said that she never managed to gallop like the cowboys' horses. She was, to put it politely, somewhat rounder and heavier.

One night Brian found the cowboys raising a pair of spotty knickers up the town flagpole. "This is our chance, Sarah!" said Brian. "Gee up!" But the cowboys leaped onto their horses and rode off before Sarah had taken a single step.

The next night, the cowboys covered over the door of the bank and painted a fake open door further down the building. Brian and Sarah set off after them again, but were soon left far behind, the sound of the cowboys' laughter fading in the distance.

But Brian never scolded his pig, because he knew she was trying her best. Each night as the cloud of dust receded behind

the escaping cowboys, he would say, "Never mind, Sarah –
you're a big help," and Sarah would snort with pleasure.

As time passed, apart from their lack of success in catching
the naughty cowboys, Brian and Sarah made a great
team. Each night, Brian would take Sarah to the
stables and feed her a huge bucket of
pigswill, and then she would settle down
for a sleep while Brian went back to his
bedroom above the sheriff's office.

But one morning, the townsfolk awoke to the sound of hooves thundering into Rusty Nail. When they looked out of their bedroom windows they saw something terrible. It was Quincy Scragbeard, the most notorious outlaw in the land. He had been terrorizing the West ever since he'd landed his treasure-filled pirate ship on the coast some years before, and then forgot where he'd parked it. Now here he was in Rusty Nail, wearing his famous black tricorne hat. He had an impossibly long black beard, which made the barber hide his scissors nervously, and his cutlass glinted in the sunlight.

"RAAAARRRRRRRRRGGGGGHHHHHHH," he roared, and the butcher fainted clean away.

Big, Sly and Wiley came out of the saloon to see where the roaring was coming from. As soon as they saw Scragbeard, they all tried to hide behind each other at once.

"I'VE COME FOR THE MONEY IN THE BANK, AND THERE'S NOTHING YOU CAN DO TO STOP ME," roared Scragbeard.

"I'm going to stop you," said Brian bravely, his voice cracking just a tiny bit.

In a blur of movement, Scragbeard lassoed Brian so that the rope pinned his arms to his sides.

"I DON'T THINK SO," said Scragbeard, grinning widely. He tramped towards the bank, shaking his head.

"YOU PEOPLE MUST BE CRAZY, LEAVING THE
DOOR OPEN LIKE—"

Crack!

Scragbeard walked straight into the fake door that the
cowboys had painted on the wall of the bank. (No one had
washed it off, as it made everyone smile whenever they walked
past it.)

There was a muffled snigger. This made Scragbeard, who
now had a large bump on his forehead, even angrier.

"I'M GOING TO GET
THE LOT OF YOU!"
he snarled. "STARTING
WITH YOU!" and
he pointed his cutlass
at Brian.

The townsfolk were horrified. They were, after all, very fond of their sheriff, despite his strange pig-riding ways.

Just then there was an unearthly, ground-shaking snort and a large pink whirlwind flew out of the stables.

Thwump!

There was now no sign of Scragbeard, except for a very squashed tricorne hat poking out from under an enormous pig. Everything was quiet for a moment, and then the entire town broke into applause.

From that day on, nobody laughed at Brian and Sarah. In fact, the townsfolk set up a statue in honour of the sheriff and the pig who saved the town that day. And Big, Sly and Wiley never caused trouble again.

Well, almost never…

BEDTIME
AT THE
LIGHTHOUSE

Philip Bell

Illustrated by

Joanne Young

It's bedtime at Nana's cottage under the lighthouse.
Lizzy and I can't sleep because Mum isn't here. It's strange
sleeping in Nana's funny little attic room.

Nana says, "I can't read any more stories. I keep falling
asleep!"

"Oh, Nana, please read one more," says Lizzy.

"Yes, Nana, please!" I say. "Just one more!"

"No, it's late, Tom," says Nana. "But I'll show you something
special instead..."

Nana turns out the light.

"But it's all dark!" says Lizzy.

"Be patient..." says Nana.

I hear the sea and the ticking clock and the telly on downstairs.

And then, suddenly, I see a shining light behind the curtains.
"The lighthouse is on!" I say.

I draw the curtains and Lizzy and I push our noses up against
the window, our breath making steamy circles.

"It's never dark living under a lighthouse!" says Lizzy,
and Nana laughs.

"Will the light come back?" I ask.

"Be patient, Tom," says Nana.

I sit and wait for the passing light from
the lighthouse.

It's bedtime at Nana's cottage under the lighthouse.

A breeze whistles through vents in the window.

Nana shuts out the draught and then kisses us both, "Goodnight, you two!"

A loud THUD makes us all jump.

"What's that?" asks Lizzy, sitting up, eyes wide.

"Windy night!" says Nana, tutting. "It's just our John taking Sealegs for a walk."

John's not our real grandad but we love him all the same. Sealegs is John's dog. He's called that because he loves to swim in the sea.

Through the window I see John carrying a torch. Sealegs jumps on the rocks under the lighthouse.

"Rooff!" says Sealegs as he runs into the night, "Rooff! Rooff!" John always tells us, "His bark is worse than his bite!"

"Can we go for a walk with Sealegs?" I ask.

"Tomorrow, Tom, tomorrow – it's bedtime now," says Nana.

"Oh, let us look for just a bit longer!" I say.

I see the glow from John's distant torch, bobbing up and down like a boat floating out at sea, as he walks into the passing light from the lighthouse.

It's bedtime at Nana's cottage under the lighthouse.

"The seagulls have gone to sleep," I say.

"But the moths are out!" says Lizzy, as a giant winged thing flaps about behind the glass.

"And the moon!" says Nana.

I look at the moonlight glittering over the sea.

"Look Nana, a ship!" says Lizzy.

"It's got hundreds of lights," I say, "It's like a floating town!"

"Do you think there are two children, 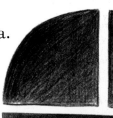 like you, trying to sleep onboard?" says Nana. "I wonder where they're going."

I imagine the children on the ship staring out of their portholes at the passing light from the lighthouse.

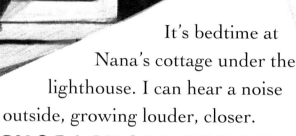

It's bedtime at
Nana's cottage under the
lighthouse. I can hear a noise
outside, growing louder, closer.

CHOPACHOPACHOPA!

"What's that, Tom?" asks Lizzy.

"Not sure," I say.

Nana's gone to make us warm milk, so we can't ask her.

CHOPACHOPACHOPA!

I see a flashing red light moving faster than a shooting star.
"Hide!" I cry.

We duck under the covers.

CHOPACHOPACHOPA!

Suddenly the duvet lifts up and Nana peers into our gloomy
cave.

"Milk's ready," she says.

I flick my torch on.

"But Nana, that noise!" squeals Lizzy.

"Yes, we're not coming out until it's gone!" I say.

Nana laughs and says, "Oh! Well, you'll not be wanting to see
a big surprise then!"

CHOPACHOPACHOPA!

In a flash, Lizzy and I throw the covers off just in time
to see a giant helicopter, striped red and white like the
lighthouse, with red flashing lights and its own
search beam pointing down to the sea.
It swoops overhead, chased by
the passing light from the
lighthouse.

It's bedtime at Nana's cottage under the lighthouse.

"Fog's coming in," says Nana.

I see wispy white air rolling in from the sea.

I hear a PEEEEEEEEEP! The sound echoes off the fog.

"What's that Nana?" I say.

"It's the foghorn, Tom," says Nana. "It's to warn passing ships in the mist to steer away from the rocks around the lighthouse."

But the foghorn doesn't bother Lizzy.

She's snuggled under the duvet, warm, asleep.

I watch her chest rise up and down like the sea, in time with the passing light from the lighthouse.

"Our John is back," says Nana. "Just in time – the

rain is setting in."

I hear John clomp up the stairs, and then he pops his head around the door. Sealegs trots in, panting, tail wagging. I lean down to stroke him. His nose is frozen cold and his fur is wet.

"Are you still up, Tom?" says John.

"He can't sleep, bless," says Nana.

John leans over the bed to kiss the sleeping Lizzy, then he gives me a giant hug. He smells of the sea and rain and wind. He says, "You wouldn't believe the things me and him have seen out on our walk. Always different, every time we go."

"I've been watching!" I say. "But I still can't sleep!"

John winks at Nana and says, "You will, you will…"

Nana strokes my hair just like Mum does.
Perhaps Mum learned it from Nana.
　　"How do you get to sleep, Nana?"
I say, snuggling close.
　　"Ah! That's easy," says Nana. "I watch
the light from the lighthouse go round and
round, round and round, round and round..."
　　"Good night, Nana," I say, yawning.
　　"Good night, Tom," says Nana,
yawning. As Nana strokes my hair,
I fall asleep and dream of
bedtime at the
lighthouse.

CELESTE,
WHO
SANG
TO THE
STARS

Kate Harper Wilson

Illustrated by
Kate Leiper

THERE WAS A TIME when the night sky was alive with stars. Not small white stars blinking in the distance, but stars of all different sizes in the brightest colours – red, green, yellow, blue – lighting up the skies like fireworks.

Leaping and dancing above the earth, they would travel wherever they pleased, swooping down low to brush the branches of trees, leaving sparkling trails of stardust on the ground.

Now, you might stop and stare at such a spectacle, but in those days it was so commonplace that people scarcely noticed the stars at all. In much the same way that you or I seldom stop to appreciate the beauty of a tree, or a butterfly's wing – so it was with the stars. They were just there, and nobody really thought about them very much.

Except, that is, for Celeste. Celeste loved the stars with all her heart. At night she would lie awake watching them through her bedroom window, singing a song her father had taught her when she was very small:

There's a special star for me in the sky
And it watches over me as I lie
And though I cannot always
see it, I haven't got a care
Because I know that it
can see me, and I know it's
always there.

When the moon was bright enough, she could see as far as the hill where she played in the summer and sledged in the winter. She would watch people as they travelled home and shut up their houses, and then she would gaze at the stars.

One night, Celeste noticed a crowd of people gathering on the hill. Perhaps they had decided to stop and enjoy the stars for once, she thought, smiling to herself.

The stars frolicked amongst the crowd, more lively even than usual, as if they were grateful for an audience. The people on the hill were dancing about with them, jigging this way and that. Celeste laughed to herself as she watched.

Until, suddenly, the dancing stopped.

As the people moved back down the hill, the stars began to dart about in panic, as if they were looking for something. Something they had lost.

And as the people from the hill came closer to the village, Celeste understood what the stars were looking for.

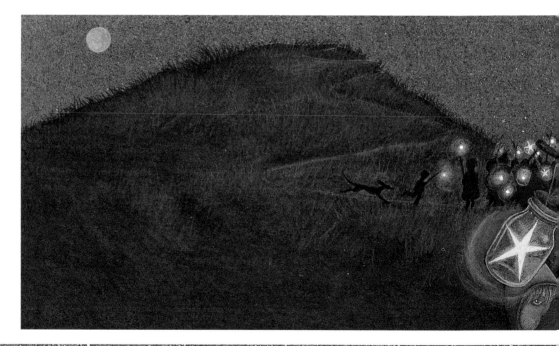

Each person was carrying a large glass jar.

And trapped inside each one, by a thick cork stopper, was a star.

Celeste banged hard on her window. "You cannot steal the stars!" she cried. "They belong in the sky! They belong with the moon and the sun and all the other stars!"

But no one heard.

The villagers carried their jars home and placed them in their gardens. Just about every house had a star on display.

People proudly told anyone passing that theirs was a Blue Star, or a Green Star, one of the rarest, or that theirs shined far more brightly than all the others.

Late at night Celeste sat by her window, but the view was quite different now. She watched sadly as the stars in the sky called to the ones in the jars. They swooped down, encouraging their imprisoned friends to fly up and come back to them, where they belonged.

But the cork stoppers were wedged in tight.

As the days went by, the stars inside the jars grew weaker. With a heavy heart, Celeste watched as they grew dimmer and dimmer until, at last, they lost their glow altogether.

The stars in the sky no longer came down, as they knew the trapped stars were lost to them. Instead they remained far away, in mourning for their friends.

Before long, the trapped stars were forgotten. A star that didn't shine was no longer a novelty, and the jars were soon covered in dirt, dust and cobwebs.

But Celeste never forgot.

One night, as she walked through the village, she

stopped at one of the abandoned jars. She knelt down to rub away a patch of dirt from the glass.

"I'm so sorry," she whispered. "I'm so sorry they did this to you."

Then something caught her eye...

She gasped. It couldn't be, could it?

It was tiny and weak, but she was sure she saw a glimmer of light!

Quickly, Celeste picked up the jar and tucked it carefully into her bag. She asked if she could take the jar, but everyone waved her away. "Take it. Take them all. They are no use to anyone now."

And so she did. She collected the jars and packed them all in her old wooden cart.

She knew exactly what she was going to do with them.

In the middle of the night, when the sky was at its blackest, she pulled the wooden cart up the hill, the faint

glow from the star in her bag helping her see the way.
When she reached the top, Celeste rubbed each jar
clean and placed it gently on the ground. The corks
were wedged tightly, but eventually she managed to
open all the jars.

Then she waited.

But nothing happened.

Then she remembered the star in her bag! She took
its cork out and placed it with the others.

She pulled her coat tight around her and waited.

And waited.

To take her mind off the cold, she sang the song her father had taught her:

There's a special star for me in the sky
And it watches over me as I lie
And though I cannot always see it, I haven't got a care
Because I know that it can see me, and I know it's always there.

Then something wonderful happened. The stars started to glow. Faintly at first, but growing stronger and stronger with every word she sang.

Celeste stared up at the tiny stars, high in the sky. They seemed to be moving. They were coming closer!

Celeste could feel the stars in the jars growing stronger. They began to shine so brightly that she felt the glass would surely melt, when suddenly, as one, they rocketed out of their jars and soared up into the sky.

Celeste laughed as all the stars danced joyously around each other, their colours more vivid than ever before.

She knew that she would remember this moment for the rest of her life.

Then, faster than anything she had ever seen, the stars
flew back to the very highest part of the sky.

Together again.

Away from the earth.

Far, far away.

And that, as you and I know, is where they remain.

And Celeste?

Celeste still watches the stars from her bedroom window.

And deep in the night, while she sleeps, a star comes by to watch over her, just as she once watched over them.

Allie
To The Rescue

Helen Yendall
Illustrated by Frann Preston-Gannon

*O*ne sunny morning, there was a new arrival at Merrydown Farm.

The pigs, hens, sheep and cows gathered round to watch as the farmer opened the truck. And out came ... the strangest animal they'd ever seen!

"It's not a sheep like me!" Sheena baaed. "Its neck is too long!"

"It's not a cow like me!" snorted Biffy. "It's too fluffy!"

"It's not a pig like me!" squeaked Prince. "It hasn't got a curly tail."

What do you think it was?

Was it a pony? Was it an elephant? Was it a giraffe?

No!

The fluffy creature walked down the ramp and looked at them.

She made an excited noise. "WARK, WARK! I'm an alpaca!" she said. "And my name is Allie. WARK, WARK!"

The animals looked at each other. An alpaca? They'd never heard of such a thing.

"I'm like a llama," Allie explained, "only smaller."

A llama? They'd never heard of such a thing. The sheep shrugged; the cows shook their heads; the hens started pecking in the yard.

Only Prince was friendly. "Come on. I'll show you round the farm," he said.

Allie was happy to have a friend. She started to hum like a bee. "HMMMMMMM…"

When they finished looking round the farm, Allie joined the other animals.

"You look funny!" said the cows. "Like a giant rabbit in a wig! And what do you do? Alpacas can't give tasty milk, like us!"

"You look funny!" said the hens. "Like a camel without a hump. Why are you here? We give the farmer delicious eggs every day. Alpacas can't do that!"

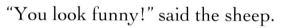

"You look funny!" said the sheep. "What are you for? We give the farmer lovely wool for knitting and making clothes. Alpacas can't do that."

But they were wrong. Allie knew her fleece was as soft as a kitten and as thick as a loaf of bread.

"You can knit lovely hats and scarves from my wool," she said.

The sheep stamped their hooves. "But there are more of us than you," Sheena said. "We can make more wool. You're not a proper farm animal."

Allie's big eyes filled with tears, so Prince quickly thought of a rhyme to cheer her up:

"An alpaca's like a little llama
Her coat is thick like woolly armour
She's the favourite of the farmer
Nasty words will never harm her!"

Allie managed to smile. "Thank you, Prince. I feel much better." She gave a little "CLICK" and a little "CLUCK".

That night, all the animals snuggled up to sleep in their usual places, but there was no room for Allie.

"I won't leave you on your own," said Prince. "Especially on your first night."

The only place left to sleep was the hard ground near the gate.

"Sorry, it's not very comfy," Prince said, as they lay down. But Allie's fur was so soft and squidgy that Prince was as warm as toast in no time at all. And he was soon fast asleep, snoring gently.

"SNNURRRRRRR, SNNURRRRRRR..."

Allie smiled. She wished the other animals would accept her like Prince had done. They thought she wasn't a proper farm animal. She knew she should try to go to sleep but she didn't feel sleepy.

The full moon was shining on the field and she could see the pigsty, the sheep asleep under the oak tree, the cows lying by the fence and all the hens on the haystack.

Then Allie pricked up her ears. She heard something! There was a noise coming from the bottom of the field.

She stood up and watched carefully. Whatever it was, it was creeping towards the hens, who were all fast asleep.

What do you think it was?

Was it a cat? Was it a dog?

No!

It was reddy-brown, with a big bushy tail. Its mouth was open and its pink tongue was hanging out. It looked very hungry.

It was a FOX!

Allie galloped as fast as she could across the field

towards it, making a loud shrieking whine: "WAAAAAAAAAA!"

The hens woke up and started clucking. "Help us, save us!" they yelled. "Help us, save us!"

But the cows were scared and stayed where they were, by the fence; the pigs were terrified and stayed safe inside the pigsty; and the sheep trembled with fear and stayed under the oak tree.

Only Allie came to the rescue.

When the fox saw Allie it stopped in its tracks – one paw raised off the ground – and stared at her. It thought she was the strangest animal it had ever seen.

Allie still wailed, "WAAAAAAAAAA!" She kicked her back legs and spat, "SPPPPPPSSSSS!" and hissed, " HSSSSSSS!"

"Go, Allie, go!" Prince yelled.

"Help us, save us!" the hens squawked, running round in circles. "Help us, save us!"

The fox backed away from Allie's kicking legs. It was scared. It had never seen anything like her.

Was it a giant rabbit in a wig? Was it a camel without a hump?

It wasn't going to stay to find out.

The fox turned and ran out of the field ... and ran and ran and ran...

"Hurrah!" the hens all cheered. "You saved us, you saved us!"

Prince came running up. "Well done, Allie. You were so brave!"

Allie smiled. Then she gave a little "CLICK" and a little "CLUCK".

All the pigs, hens, sheep and cows gathered round her.

"We're sorry, Allie," snorted Biffy. "We shouldn't have laughed at you just because you look different."

"And we should have made you welcome when you arrived this morning," said Sheena.

All the animals felt bad. They hung their heads down.

"Will you stay and protect us from the fox every night – please?" said Prince.

"Am I a proper farm animal?" said Allie. The hens, cows, sheep and pigs all shouted "YEEEEESSSSS!" as loudly as they could.

Allie smiled and nodded. "Then I will." And then she made a humming noise like a bee "HMMMMMMMMMM!" And she gave a small "CLICK" and a small "CLUCK."

And you know what that means – don't you?

PRINCESS IMOGEN'S INDEPENDENT DAY

Christine O'Neill

Illustrated by Sara Gibbeson

FROM MORNING TO NIGHT Princess Imogen
had people fussing over her. But one day she
told them all to

STOP!

The ladies of the bedchamber came to get Princess Imogen dressed. She squeezed her fists tight and told them to

STOP! I CAN DO IT MYSELF!

Imogen pushed and she pulled, she wiggled and she wriggled, until the royal clothes were on … inside out. "I like it this way. Inside out is the smartest way to dress."

Two footmen chased Princess Imogen to the back door, holding out her red boots. She spun around and told them to

STOP! I CAN DO IT MYSELF!

Imogen twisted and she turned, she stamped and she stomped, until the royal boots were on … the wrong feet. "I like it this way. Swapped over boots will splash the best."

A stable boy stood by a pony, ready to lift Princess Imogen onto its back. She folded her arms and told him to

STOP! I CAN DO IT MYSELF!

Imogen struggled and she stretched, she climbed and she clambered, until she sat on the royal saddle … facing backwards. "I like it this way. Back to front riding is always the bounciest."

The King's knight saw Princess Imogen stuck in a tree and rushed to her rescue. She took a deep breath and told him to

STOP! I CAN DO IT MYSELF!

Imogen hung and she swung, she flopped and she dropped, until her royal bottom was on the ground … in a muddy puddle. "I like it this way. Squelchy mud is simply the softest."

Five housemaids with sponges and soap tried to catch Princess Imogen and give her a bath. She dodged round each one and told them to

STOP! I CAN DO IT MYSELF!

Imogen trickled and she tipped, she swirled and she swooshed, until the royal bath was full … of foam. "I like it like this. Bubble baths clean the most royal of messes."

The Queen had heard about her daughter's
independent day and gave Princess Imogen a book
to read all by herself. Imogen grabbed the
Queen's hand and told her to

STOP!
I CAN'T DO IT ALONE.

Imogen tugged and she hugged, she cuddled and she snuggled, until the royal storybook was open … for a proper bedtime story. "I like it this way," Imogen sleepily said. "Everyone knows that shared stories have the happiest ever afters."

THE
DANCING BEAR

Suzy Robinson

Illustrated by
Gemma O'Callaghan

IT WAS SO COLD that the village pond had frozen over. Children with their skates of whittled bone swept across the ice, shrieking and laughing, pushing, chasing, and often falling down.

The big black bear tied up outside the tavern sat upright, watching them enviously. He imagined himself with them, sliding over the glistening pond, joining their games. "I would be good at that," he thought. "I should feel the wind in my fur. I wouldn't be cold if I could rush about with the children." He shook himself and a cloud of snow flew off his back, and the chain which held him fast, from his collar to a wooden post, rattled furiously.

Some of the children standing by the pond, their skates in their hands, saw the bear shaking off the snow. They laughed and pointed, and some of them ran at him, pelting him with snowballs. The bear did not mind. He wanted to be part of their fun, but he would rather be free to skate with them and kick snow back at them with his large hairy paws. He laughed and opened his jaws wide, showing huge, sparkling teeth. But the children heard only growling and ran away frightened, some crying with fear.

"No," the bear tried to say to them, "No, don't go away," and he raised his paws in the air to show that he would not hurt them. They cried all the harder, running home now that the game was spoiled. The bear curled up on the ground, tucking his wicked paws under him, hiding the claws which had so frightened the children.

He had arrived early that morning, brought by merchants on a painted wagon, hung about with ribbons of all colours rippling in the wintry breeze. Today was the Fair, and now everyone gathered to see plays and pageants, watch the jugglers and fire-eaters, and listen to the jongleurs sing their songs. There were stalls with every kind of sweetmeat, dancing and games. A stove had been set up near the bear roasting chestnuts, their delicious smell wafting through the air. The bear could feel the warmth, but he shivered, his paws very cold on the frozen ground.

Three men approached him and prodded him with a stick. They led him to the stage and people gathered around, stamping their feet: "Dance, bear, dance!"

The men poked him until he lumbered up and danced. The crowd clapped louder, and even children who had cloaked themselves in their mothers' skirts began to laugh with glee.

The bear felt proud because he was the centre of attention, and danced faster, holding his paws up in the air. But the men wanted him to roar as he danced, so they hit him. It hurt the bear and he growled, not in anger but in pain. The crowd cheered, but the bear was tired and cold and his back hurt from the sticks.

Finally the crowd became bored, and drifted off to see what other entertainments there were. One little girl remained when the others had gone. She held a basket of apples and, stepping forward, she offered one to the bear. The men shooed her away, shouting at her, and she dropped the apple as she fled.

One of the men led the bear back to the tavern and hooked his chain over the post once more. Meanwhile, the bear had picked up the fallen apple secretly and had stowed it in his cheek for safe-keeping, so when at last he was left alone, he crunched it up happily and was grateful to the little girl.

The sounds of laughing echoed across the village as the people enjoyed the Fair. Men and women sang bawdy songs while they drank ale in the tavern, and a dog sat lazily in a doorway, gnawing on a bone. Nobody took any notice of the bear. The snow had started to fall again, landing on his head and

back, covering him with a frosty whiteness. Then he saw the apple-girl again, walking towards him with her basket. Her head was bare even in this cold weather and she had only one thin blanket over her dress. On her feet she wore broken shoes. The bear huddled on the ground and tried to look smaller and less fierce because he did not want the girl to be afraid of him and go away. She was not afraid and went closer, laying her basket down in front of him. Then she took the blanket from her thin shoulders and laid it carefully over the bear's wide, furry back.

"No," said the bear, "I have a thick coat. You have nothing. You must not give me your blanket."

But the little girl just smiled and sat down beside him, and took apples from her basket, giving one to him and eating another herself. She looked up at the bear, smiling as if expecting a story.

"I come from a country far away from here," said the bear dreamily. "It is warm and sunny, although sometimes it rains for days, and then the fields flood and the roads run like rivers. Everybody smiles, though, even when it rains, and they dress in colourful garments and eat colourful foods. Boys and girls carry baskets on their heads, full not just of apples, but of sweet oranges and pineapples and bananas. And I danced for them because I wanted to, because it made the children smile and throw pretty flowers at me. No one beat me with sticks, or prodded me with branches; they danced with me and everybody sang.

"But one day some men came and put chains on me, and took me away. I travelled with them over thirsty deserts and tall, snow-capped mountains. Everywhere we stopped, I danced for the crowds. But the men hit me and poked at my head until I was sore, and I wept for my home. Now here I am with you; it is snowing, and we are both cold."

The little girl looked down and smiled, and edged closer to him, to his shaggy black coat.

The day was ending and the pond was soon deserted. The stove cooking chestnuts was doused, and the stage, with its poles and flags, was taken down and driven away in the coloured wagon. The watery sun was sinking and glowing pink, staining the snow and the ice.

"Oh, how I would like to skate," said the bear. "How I would love to be free to feel the wind in my fur. I would dance and skate until the end of the world. I wouldn't mind the cold if I could play on the frozen pond, no, I wouldn't mind at all."

The little girl beside him rose to her knees and, putting her arms around the bear's great neck, she undid his heavy metal collar. Then she got up and walked a few paces, stretched out her hand to the bear and beckoned to him. He stood up cautiously and padded towards her, not quite believing that he was leaving his chain behind. They walked together to the pond.

The bear was so excited, he launched himself vigorously onto the ice, skidding but whooping with joy. He fell, sprawling, and slid a little way, and the girl came laughing up behind him, she too falling down. There they were, a heap of legs and paws

and fur. They both got up and tried again, this time balancing well. The little girl clung to the bear and he pulled her along as he skated on all four feet. They laughed as they slid across the pond and went round and round, faster and faster, the wind blowing their fur and hair. The bear had never been so happy. He felt he might burst for joy, with his new friend clinging tightly to him.

Gingerly he got up onto his back legs and started balancing upright; he began skating again, skimming the pond and dancing a graceful dance. Even though it was so cold, they both shouted and laughed as they had never laughed before.

There they remained joyfully, hand in paw, as the sun set, as the moon smiled on them its silvery smile, and then as the dawn broke with the thrilling song of the first birds.

THEO TODD,
11 BELTON RD,
BATH,
SOMERSET,
BA17 6JK
UNITED KINGDOM

A Parcel for Theo

Claire McCauley

Illustrated by **Cate James**

"PARCEL FOR YOU, THEO," Mum called, "from Uncle Joe."

Theo took the stairs two at a time and jumped the final four, but slowed as he reached the rectangular package on the hall table. He lifted it gently and held it to his ear. No rattle, bang or hiss. "It doesn't feel dangerous enough," he said.

"Well, I did ask him never to send indoor fireworks again," said Mum. She turned to grab the fire extinguisher. "But just in case..."

Theo squeezed the parcel. It was soft – squishy, even. He tore off the brown wrapping, unfurled the blue tissue paper and looked down at the last thing he expected to get from his explorer uncle.

A cuddly toy. It was shaped like a cat, but had a much growlier face.

"That's a jaguar," Mum said. "What a lovely toy!"

Theo looked from the jaguar, whose fur was the colour of buttered toast, to Mum, and back again. "I love him!"

Mum picked up her camera. "Smile," she said.

Theo wanted to send Uncle Joe a thank you letter in a proper envelope. But explorers don't stay in one place for long, so the only way to contact Uncle Joe was by email. Mum helped him type a message, then attached the photo she'd taken of Theo cuddling Jaguar.

Theo and Jaguar became the best of friends. They went everywhere together until the day of Theo's first swimming lesson. He left Jaguar guarding his clothes in the changing room. When he and Mum returned, Jaguar wasn't there. Theo searched the lockers, the bin and under the bench, but he was gone.

They hurried to the reception desk and Mum explained what had happened.

"What does it look like?" asked the lady.

"He's brownish and soft and medium-sized and answers to the name Jaguar," said Theo.

He wasn't in lost property, so Mum left their phone number in case he turned up later. That night, Theo cried. He couldn't get to sleep for ages without Jaguar.

The next day, Theo saw reminders of Jaguar everywhere. A girl in the park had hair that curled just like Jaguar's fur. There was a jungle that Jaguar would have loved in a book in the library.

By teatime, Theo's tummy felt too wobbly for food. As he explained this to Mum, the phone rang. Mum rushed to answer, then flashed a smile at Theo. "Uncle Joe!" she mouthed, before turning back to the phone. "Yes, he loved Jaguar, but he's lost him now and—"

Theo grabbed the phone. "Hello? Uncle Joe?"

"Hi, short stuff," boomed his uncle. "So your mum thinks that Jaguar is lost?"

Theo forgot that Uncle Joe couldn't see him, and nodded.

"But you and I know that he's not a lost kind of animal, don't we?"

"Where is he, then?" Theo asked in a tiny voice.

"Well, I don't exactly know," Uncle Joe admitted, "but I mentioned my travels when I wrapped him up and I wonder if that didn't put an idea into his head."

Theo took a deep breath. "I suppose he might have gone exploring, like you. That's better than being lost, right?"

"Much better. The adventures are amazing, and after all, jaguars are wild animals."

Theo gulped. "They are?"

"Of course they are. I don't send you safe things, remember? That Jaguar has a streak of danger in him, that's for sure. Now, perhaps you could look at a map, see where he might have gone to explore."

Theo passed the phone back to Mum and heaved the atlas down from the bookcase. He searched for places where Jaguar might have gone.

Theo spent every spare moment of the week examining the atlas. He was far too busy to be sad that Jaguar was away.

ATLAS OF THE WORLD

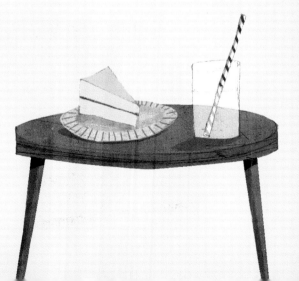

On Saturday, as he ate his cereal, the post clattered through the letterbox. He scooped up two letters for Mum, and a postcard which had his name at the top. A picture of a huge waterfall was on the other side. Theo and Mum read the message.

Dear Theo,
Having a wonderful time exploring the Amazon and wrestling grouchy crocodiles. Have fun and eat up your veg.
See you soon,
love Jaguar

Theo Todd,
11 Belton Road,
Bath,
Somerset,
BA17 6JK,
United Kingdom

A few days later another postcard arrived. As Mum read it out, Theo studied the picture of a rainforest.

Dear Theo,
Having great fun hypnotizing snakes and spiders. I won't bring any home with me though. Be good for Mum. See you soon,
love Jaguar

Theo Todd,
11 Belton Road,
Bath,
Somerset,
BA17 6JK,
United Kingdom

Then Mum's mobile rang. She scrabbled to answer it, then sprang up and strode out of the room. When she returned, Theo asked for his crayons, and drew a picture of Jaguar at a tea party with lots of jungle animals.

The next morning, Mum called up to him. "PARCEL FOR YOU, THEO."

He trudged down the stairs, convinced that no parcel would ever be as good as the one in which he got Jaguar.

He frowned when he saw Mum's empty hands. "Shall I wait for you to get the fire extinguisher?"

Mum shook her head. "It isn't from Uncle Joe," she said.

Theo scratched his head and wondered who else would send him something. Mum helped him slice along the package with scissors. He ripped the cardboard open.

THEO TODD,
11 BELTON RD,
BATH,
SOMERSET.
BA17 6JK
UNITED KINGDOM

Inside lay Jaguar. Theo squealed. "He's finished exploring and posted himself home! What a clever Jaguar!"

He hugged Jaguar, then Mum, then Jaguar again. As he did, a familiar scent tickled his nose. "But why does he smell of the swimming pool?"

Mum's eyes were wide. "Erm ... I guess he did a lot of swimming while he was away."

THE NIGHT THIEF
AND THE
MOON

Katherine Latham

Illustrated by Elisa Mac

HIS DARK BLUE FUR bristled in the cold evening breeze. The thief curled his spiny fingers over the edge of his burrow and sniffed the cool air. He opened his gummy eyes. His long black lashes slowly came unstuck, thick with the sleep of a

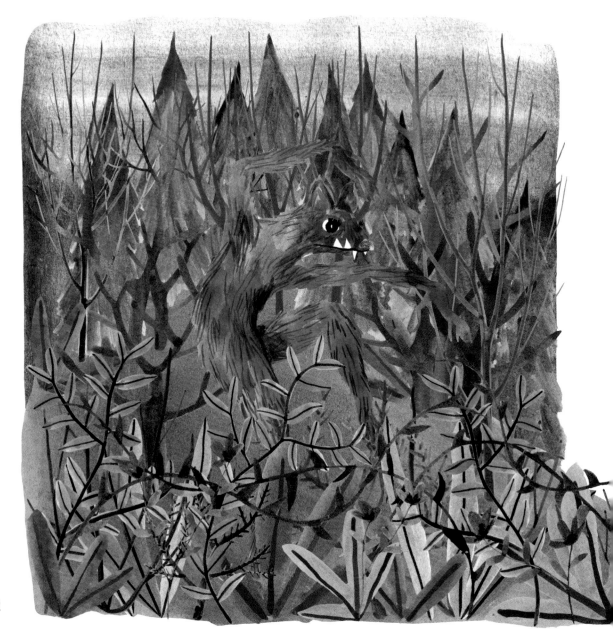

hundred years. The sun was low on the horizon and shone bright pink in his great round eyes. He flinched away from the light. He was too early.

The thief slid backwards, deep into his nest of leaves, and snuggled into his warm pit. He wriggled his wrinkled nose, yawned a great black hole of a yawn, and stretched his front paws, then his back paws, until he was lying flat on his bony ribs, stretched out in the dirt. He licked his lips, revealing jagged canines, and flicked his big, hollow ears. Spying a wandering woodlouse, this strange blue creature smacked it up with his long grey tongue and crunched it with delight.

Now, just a shadow against the darkening night sky, the thief dragged his scrawny body from his bed, pulled on his tatty old pinstriped jacket, turned up his collar, grabbed his fishing net and crept from his leafy home.

The forest stretched into the darkness and the trees reached their long arms to the sky. Their bare fingers, spread wide, were tipped with frost. The dimming light cast long shadows and a gentle breeze plucked the last brown leaves into the air.

High in the branches, yellow eyes blinked and turned to stare at the thief. One owl screeched as he drew near, then another, then another, until a wailing choir could be heard far away on the wind.

The thief stood defiantly. He shook his fishing net at his watchers and threw his head back with a rasping laugh. Then he took off through the forest, dancing through the shadows.

The thief pushed his way through thickets and brambles until he broke from the undergrowth onto a muddy path, his blue fur now tangled with thorns and twigs. He could just make out a sliver of light from the rising moon. One solitary star shone brightly above him.

The thief lifted his net and leaped with all his might. He jumped high into the sky, just making it above the tops of the highest trees.

SWISH!

Landing heavily on the dirt path, the star shone brightly in his filthy paws. He shoved it carelessly into one of his many pockets

and the light was gone.

As the hour grew late, twinkling star after twinkling star popped into view. A crescent moon now hung lazily on the horizon.

The muddy path turned into gravel, then a quiet road, twisting and turning to a distant town high up on a hill. The thief hopped along the road. He jigged and skipped and sniggered. Then he leaped high into the sky.

SWISH!

With another star in his pocket, the sky became a little darker. Soon the creature was dancing past streets and houses. Sweet-smelling smoke billowed from chimneys, curtains were shut tight and all was quiet.

A fluffy white cat shot across the road and stopped in its tracks when it spied the shadowy creature. It arched its back and hissed. The thief raised its deep blue hackles, bared its wonky teeth and hissed right back. The cat turned on its heels and fled in terror. The thief leaped into the sky with glee.

SWISH!

The sky became a little darker. He had jumped as high as the rooftops to catch this small twinkly star, and as he fell he saw a curtain twitch and a tiny pink nose press hard against the window. The boy threw his window wide and pointed accusingly at the thief. His breath hung like a cloud on the cold air.

"Thief!" he cried. The dark blue shadow saluted to the boy and bowed, then chuckled and continued on his way.

Springing and cavorting, up winding streets and cobbled steps, the thief came to the centre of the town high on the hill. He looked up in wonder at the stars blinking in the clear night sky. He licked his lips and flicked his ears.

Running through the narrow streets and alleyways, he jigged and hopped and swished! Little by little the sky became darker and darker.

The thief passed white cottages covered in roses, grand town houses and tiny bungalows. Everywhere he went windows were thrown open and children in pyjamas and nighties cried, "Rascal!" and "Crook!"

But the thief paid no attention. He cackled and chortled as he leaped high into the sky.

SWISH!

One by one he bundled the stars into his pockets. Each time the sky became a little darker. He danced and swished until there was nothing left but the sliver of the moon hanging vulnerable, alone in the shadowy night.

Looking up, the thief licked his lips and flicked his ears. Then he crouched … took a deep breath … and leaped as high as he could!

SWISH!

He bundled the moon into his pocket
and all the light was gone. Only blackness
remained, too dark even for shadows.
Now invisible in the night, the thief
heard gasps of horror all around him.
The children began to cry, mourning
the terrible loss of the stars and
the moon. The thief sniggered to
himself in the shadows. Then…

ZIP!

A star shot into the air and
spiralled gently downwards.

FIZZLE! POP!

More stars burst upwards.
They split into a thousand
pink lights and floated
peacefully until they
came to rest in the sky.

In the dim light the children squinted, leaning out of their windows as far as they dared, searching for the thief. The dark blue shadow unbuttoned his jacket and opened it wide.

WOOSH! ZIP! ZOOOOOOM!

The most magnificent fireworks erupted from the tiny town on the hill. They whizzed and popped and fizzed and the night sky lit up with dancing stars. The thief hopped and jigged and his big black eyes shone blue and pink and white. The children looked on in wonder. They began to laugh and clap, then they hopped and danced with joy. Then…

BOOM!

The moon sprang from the thief's pocket and rushed into the sky, spinning like a boomerang. It whistled as it waltzed amongst the stars, from one side of the night sky to the other, up then down, round and round. Finally it settled, reclining as though exhausted, hanging lazily on the horizon.

The children were transfixed. They didn't take their eyes from the spectacle in the sky. They didn't notice the strange dark blue creature buttoning up his jacket, turning up his collar and sloping out of the town.

The thief licked his lips and flicked his ears. He jogged wearily back down the hill, along the wooded path to his burrow. The owls winked at him as he passed. He saluted them and bowed, then sniggered and continued on his way.

Settling back into his warm nest of leaves, the thief felt something jagged digging into his side. A small twinkly star was stuck in his knotted fluff. He pulled it free and let the light glow in his great round eyes. Then...

FLIT! ZZZZZZZZZZZZZZ!

The tiny star darted into the sky, fluttering over the treetops and out of sight. A sprinkling of icy stardust drifted down from its tail. The thief shivered. He tucked his paws under his body, poked his nose into the blue fur of his chest and closed his big black eyes. He settled in to a deep sleep, twitching his paws as he dreamed of waltzing with the moon on its celestial stage.

A hundred years later the thief's deep blue fur bristled in the cold evening breeze as he curled his spiny fingers over the edge of his burrow and sniffed the cool air. Slowly he opened his gummy eyes. His long black lashes came unstuck, thick with sleep. The sun was low on the horizon and shone bright pink in his great round eyes. He flinched away from the light. He was too early…

The End